MW00948509

www.ingoblumbooks.com
Published by planetOh concepts gmbh
www.planetohconcepts.com

ISBN: 978-1-982941-74-1

Cover and chapter Illustrations by Antonio Pahetti
Copy design and book layout by Emy Farella

INGO BLUM

Where Is My Little Dragon?

Illustrated by Antonio Pahetti

planetOh
concepts

Where is Amy, my little dragon?

She is not in the castle.

Is she guarding the princess?

No, she is not there.

She is not in the supermarket.

She must not want to buy anything.

Is she with the other dragons?

No, she is not there either.

Can she spit fire?

Like in a fairy tale?

Sure she can.
Look!

Is she helping a brave knight?

No, that is another dragon!

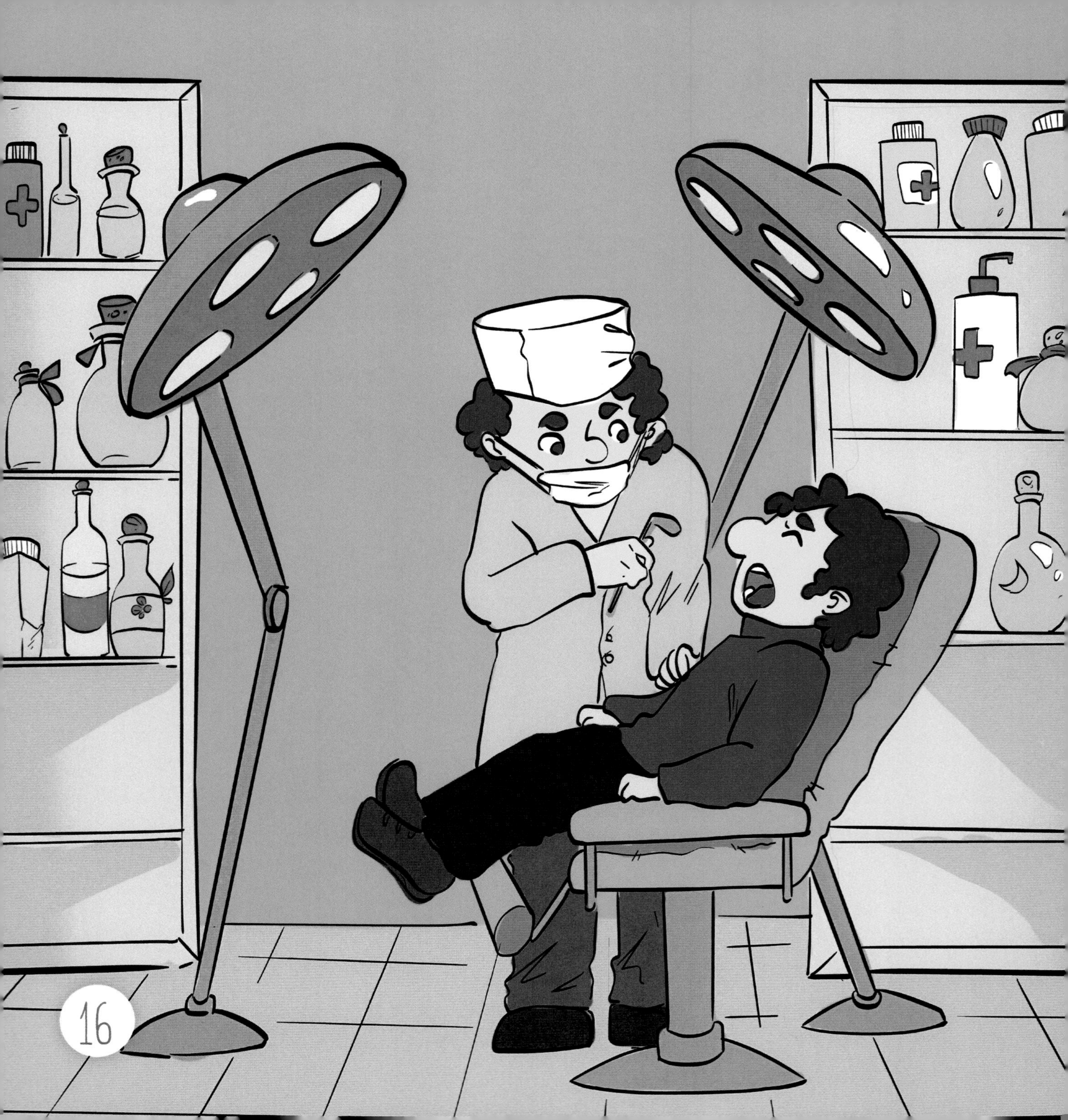

Is she at the dentist?

She does not have a toothache.

She is not sick at all.

She is not in the attic.

That is only a toy dragon on the shelf.

Look, there she is!

Amy is flying through the air.

We found her!

Goodbye, Amy!

Amy the Drago

More Reading and Coloring Fun

ISBN 978-1-982942-12-0

ISBN 978-1-982941-28-4

ISBN 978-1-982941-88-8

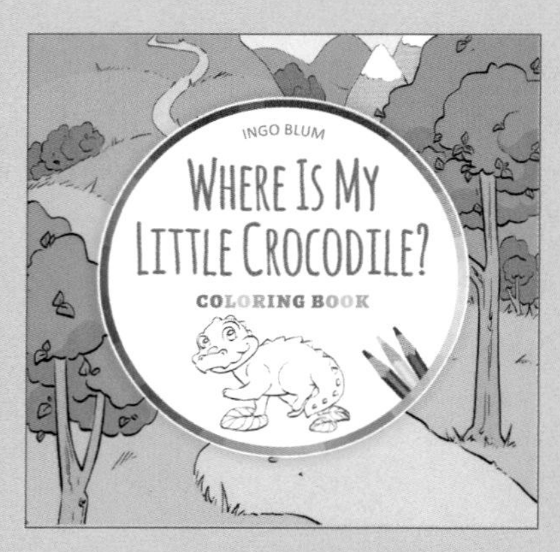

ISBN 978-3-947410-21-7

ISBN 978-3-947410-23-1

ISBN 978-3-947410-25-5

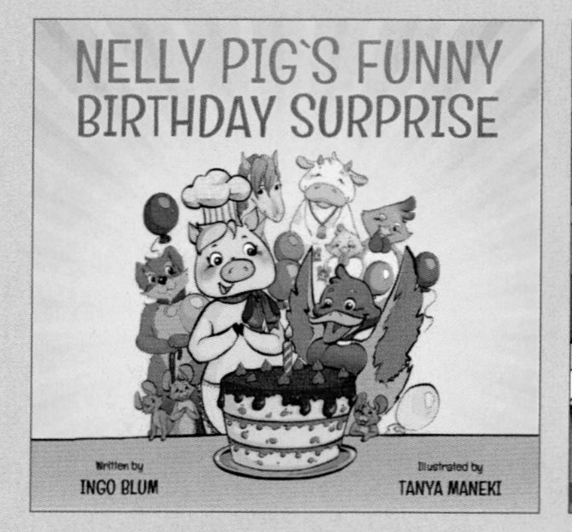

ISBN 978-1-983075-91-9

ISBN 978-1-982958-22-0

ISBN 978-3-947410-56-9

Thank You

Thank you for reading this little story. I hope you enjoyed it the same way I did while writing it. If you would like to know when my next book comes out, find more books I have written, and receive some occasional updates from me, just visit me on my website.

Do you find reader reviews helpful? If so, please spare a moment to help me by rating this book, so others will find it (and read it!), too. I always appreciate an honest review on Amazon.

RATE NOW

Looking forward to your comments, and opinions.

About the Author

Ingo Blum is a German author and comedian. His journey to become a children's book author began during his day job. He has always enjoyed projects where he could create artwork for kids. He started writing stories to accompany these projects for fun, and with some encouragement from friends and family (and their kids!) he decided to share his stories with the world. Ingo works with international illustrators, with whom he constantly develops new concepts and stories.

About the Illustrator

Antonio Pahetti is a young artist with a lot of experience in children's illustration, who makes his illustrations with much love and a passion for details. His works are published in many countries. He lives in the Ukraine.

Made in the USA
Las Vegas, NV
15 May 2022

48932475R00021